MAGICAL TALES FROM THE JUNGLE BOOK

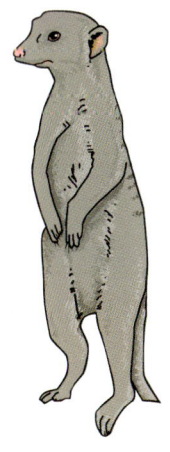

6-in-1 Series
Magical Tales from the Jungle Book

ISBN: 978-93-5049-444-8

Printed in 2017

© Shree Book Centre

Retold by
Sunita Pant Bansal

Published by

Shree Book Centre

8, Kakad Industrial Estate, S. Keer Marg, off L. J. Road
Matunga (west), Mumbai 400 016, India
Tel: +91-22-2437 7516 / 2437 4559 / 2438 0907
Fax: +91-22-2430 9183
Email: sales@shreebookcentre.com
Website: **www.shreebookcentre.com**

Contents

Preface

The Jungle Book, written by Nobel laureate Rudyard Kipling in 1894, is one of the most loved children's books in the world. Kipling has used animal characters to impart important lessons in life such as discipline, friendship, bravery, helping people and respecting elders.

The central theme of the Jungle Book revolves around a boy Mowgli, who was raised by wolves and educated by a bear, a panther and a python in an Indian jungle.

This volume contains fascinating stories about a strong elephant and his young mahout, a family of seals, and a brave mongoose. It is well known that elephants display human-like emotions such as joy, anger, grief, compassion and love, but in the *Jungle Book,* they can dance too!

Magical Tales from the Jungle Book contains six carefully picked stories, accompanied by lively and colourful illustrations. The stories are written in simple language for easy comprehension. The speech bubbles will help children understand what the characters think and feel. The glossary at the end of the book will enrich children's vocabulary.

The Elephant Dance

Long long ago, elephants were used by the British government for transportation. Once a mahout named Big Toomai and his son, Little Toomai, were employed by the British to look after a strong elephant named Kala Nag. It was Little Toomai's duty to keep a watch on the elephant at night.

But Little Toomai yearned to be a mahout like his father.

So, he told his father, "Father, can I be Kala Nag's mahout? He is happy and well-behaved when he is with me. Besides, I take care of him very well."

Big Toomai did not want to dishearten his son.

He said, "The government owns Kala Nag. Express your wish to Bade Sahib, the highest ranking official of this area. He decides who becomes the mahout of the elephants."

Little Toomai went to Bade Sahib's office and waited outside patiently. When he was called inside, Little Toomai expressed his desire to Bade Sahib. The official was impressed.

He said, "Kala Nag is a big elephant. So I cannot let you ride him. However, I will give you a coin as I am proud of you."

Little Toomai asked him, "But when can I ride Kala Nag?"

Bade Sahib said jokingly, "Well, you can ride Kala Nag the day you see the elephants dance."

Later in the day, Little Toomai asked his father curiously, "When will the elephants dance?"

Big Toomai answered, "Son, the elephants never dance. Maybe Bade Sahib meant that you can never ride Kala Nag."

Little Toomai was disappointed.

With a heavy heart, he started feeding Kala Nag and keeping a watch on the other elephants.

Soon Little Toomai fell asleep. Suddenly, a loud noise woke him up. He saw Kala Nag walking towards the forest. Little Toomai followed the elephant to a pond.

Kala Nag stopped at the pond where hundreds of wild and tamed elephants had gathered in the moonlight. Bade Sahib's elephant, Pudmini, was also present.

It was an amazing sight for Little Toomai, as the elephants stomped their feet and danced merrily. He could not believe his eyes.

The elephants danced and played all night by the pond. Then, just before dawn, Kala Nag and Pudmini returned home.

The next morning, Little Toomai rushed to Bade Sahib's office. Excitedly, he narrated all that he had seen the previous night.

Bade Sahib did not believe him and laughed. "Are you making this up because

I said you can ride Kala Nag only if you see the elephants dance?" asked Bade Sahib.

Little Toomai replied, "If you don't believe me, please send your men to the pond where the elephants danced all night. Your men can see for themselves."

Bade Sahib sent some of his men with Little Toomai to find out the truth.

Bade Sahib's men came back and reported what they saw to their boss. An old mahout said, "We found the footprints of Kala Nag and Pudmini from the shelter to the forest pond. In fact, the plants and trees near the pond were trampled and broken too. The devastation must have happened because of the elephants' dancing."

Bade Sahib asked them, "Are you trying to say that the elephants actually danced?"

The mahout replied, "I have lived here for the past seventy years. Many years ago, I too have seen the elephants dance."

Bade Sahib was shocked. He promised Little Toomai that he could ride Kala Nag when he turned eighteen.

When Little Toomai grew up, he became a good mahout who looked after the elephants well. He was respected by everyone for his knowledge of the forest and the elephants. The elephants loved him too.

Sea Catch's Family

Long ago, there was a beautiful island called Novastoshnah in the Bering Sea near Alaska. In summer, thousands of seals came to the island in search of food. One summer, a big seal named Sea Catch came to Novastoshnah.

Sea Catch was young and had grey fur. He fought with many sea animals and won too. Hence, he was considered the strongest among the seals. Unfortunately, he had no friends.

Once, Sea Catch found a nice spot on the beach and started living there. But he longed for company.

One evening, Sea Catch saw a sleek and beautiful seal named Matkah near his house, while he was returning home from the sea. As he was curious by nature, he asked Matkah, "Were you trying to steal something from my house?"

Matkah was surprised. So she asked him, "Why do you think I am a thief?"

Seeing Sea Catch speechless, Matkah continued, "I was admiring your lovely house. Don't blame anyone without any reason."

Realising his mistake, Sea Catch apologised to Matkah, "Please forgive me and join me for dinner. I have caught many fish today."

Matkah forgave him and agreed to stay for dinner.

Soon, Sea Catch and Matkah became good friends. They spent all their free time together. As time passed, they fell in love and got married. They had a great summer on the island of Novastoshnah. When winter came, they went away from the island.

The following summer, Sea Catch returned to Novastoshnah much before his wife arrived there. He set up a lovely and safe house for them to stay in. When Matkah came back, she was overjoyed to see her new home.

After a few weeks, Matkah delivered a baby. She said, "Look, our baby is white in colour, my dear husband."

Sea Catch was unhappy because he wanted the baby to be grey just like him.

"The baby should be strong and intelligent like you. His colour does not matter," said Matkah, cheering him up.

Sea Catch understood what Matkah meant. He named his baby Kotick and played with him all day.

Matkah said, "Now, does it matter that our baby is white?" Sea Catch was embarrassed. He replied, "No, I love him a lot."

When Kotick grew up, Sea Catch and Matkah often left him on the beach to play with the other baby seals and went out to the sea to catch fish. Kotick always wanted to accompany his parents as he loved the sea.

But his mother did not allow him to come with them.

One morning, as usual, Kotick's parents left for the sea. Kotick complained to a baby seal, "I wonder why my mother stops me from going into the sea." The baby seal said, "Don't listen to her. Do as you wish." Kotick replied, "Yes, you are right!"

Kotick dived into the deep sea. It was a new experience for him, as his parents allowed him to play only in the shallow waters.

Kotick had a lot of fun in the deep waters of the sea. He thought, "I am not as weak as my mother thinks."

After some time, Kotick decided to return to the beach. But a huge wave carried him deeper into the sea. He accidentally hit his head against a rock and began to drown. Fortunately, Matkah saw him and saved him. She scolded Kotick, "Why didn't you listen to my advice and instructions?"

Kotick apologised to his mother, "I am sorry. I will be careful from now on."

Matkah promised her son, "I will teach you to swim in the deep waters when you are ready for the challenges of the sea. Till then, be patient." Kotick agreed to wait.

Special Kotick

In the winters, the seals migrated from the island of Novastoshnah. "Son, we have to leave this place now," Matkah told her son Kotick.

On the way to the new place, Matkah taught Kotick how to sleep on his back in the water and catch many varieties of fishes such as cod and halibut.

After a long journey, Kotick and his parents reached their destination. Kotick saw many seals there. They shouted and welcomed him, "You are a holluschickie now!"

Kotick was confused. "What did you say now?" he asked them.

They answered, "Holluschickie is a bachelor or a young male seal."

Saying so, the seals went to a meeting headed by the oldest seal. His name was Chief. Chief said, "This place is different from Novastoshnah, as there are men here. You must learn the ways of the new place."

Chief then looked at Kotick and asked him, "How did you manage to get white fur?"

"I was born with white fur," said Kotick.

Chief was quite amused by this. He said, "Then you have to be extra careful because you are special."

Kotick promised, "Don't worry, Chief! I will take good care of myself."

You are special, so be extra careful.

One morning, the seals were resting on the beach. Then, all of a sudden, they saw two men. They cried in fear, "They have come to take us away!"

Men used the skin of seals to make leather.

The two men started driving the seals just like how sheep were herded for wool shearing.

Many of the seals left quietly with the two men, without protesting. When one of the men wanted to take Kotick, the other man shouted, "Stop! Seals are never white in colour. Let us run before he kills us. He must be the ghost of a seal we killed in the past."

Hearing this, Kotick was thankful for his white colour.

Soon after the men left, Kotick asked the other seals, "Why didn't those seals retaliate against the men?"

"This has been happening for ages. No one can change it. You are lucky that they did not take you," said one of the seals.

Hearing this, Kotick became very upset.

Kotick was kind and cared for everyone's safety and welfare. He just couldn't bear to see his companions leave him. So he followed them quietly.

The men stopped after half an hour and took the seals they had captured into a big building. Hiding himself, Kotick saw the men kill the seals and then peel off their skin.

Kotick had never seen anything so cruel and terrible. He immediately went home and told his father Sea Catch about this.

"We are helpless, son. We cannot save ourselves from the men. They are stronger and smarter than us," said Sea Catch.

Kotick suggested, "Then let us move to a safer place, father."

Sea Catch nodded sadly and said, "I am afraid there is no such place. We will find men everywhere."

A sea walrus overheard them. He intervened, "The sea cows know places where the men will not be able to disturb you. They can guide you to one such place."

Kotick went in search of the sea cows. He found them in a faraway ocean after many days.

He followed them to a long sandy beach on an island, which seemed suitable for seal nurseries. He knew by the feel of the water that the men had never come there. There were many fish in the water.

Kotick was overjoyed as his hard work had paid off. He thought, "This place is ten times better than our place. The men cannot come down the cliffs, and the rocks will prevent the ships from coming here. This is the safest place for seals."

Kotick could not wait to tell the other seals about this and he rushed back home.

The Seals Move to Safety

Kotick wanted to ensure the safety of all the seals and bring them to the new island. So he swam as fast as he could for six days to tell his family about the new island.

Kotick's mother, Matkah, was delighted to see him.

Matkah asked him eagerly, "Did you find a safe place for us?" Kotick replied, "Yes! I will tell you all about the new place."

Meanwhile, when Kotick was away, Matkah had chosen a lovely seal named Lary for Kotick to marry. She said, "Kotick, I want you to meet Lary first."

Kotick went to the beach to meet Lary.

Lary was very intelligent. Kotick liked her a lot and decided to marry her.

Then he met his father Sea Catch and greeted him. He said, "Father, please organise a meeting this evening. I have something important to announce."

Sea Catch immediately called all the seals for a meeting.

Kotick addressed them, "As you all know, I have been looking for a safe place for the seals to live in. Now, I have found such a place and I request you all to move there."

All the seals laughed at Kotick. They said, "There is no such place, Kotick. You are dreaming an impossible dream."

When Kotick turned to his father for support, Sea Catch was laughing too. Kotick was very sad and upset. So he went home quietly.

On his way back, he met a young seal who teased him, "Kotick, how come you decided to get married? I thought you would spend the rest of your life prowling in the sea."

Kotick retorted, "It is a shame that none of you understand why I spent the last few days in the sea. It was for everyone's benefit. Leave me alone! I will knock you down if you don't get out of my way."

The young seal challenged Kotick to a fight. He said to Kotick, "I will come to your new island if you beat me."

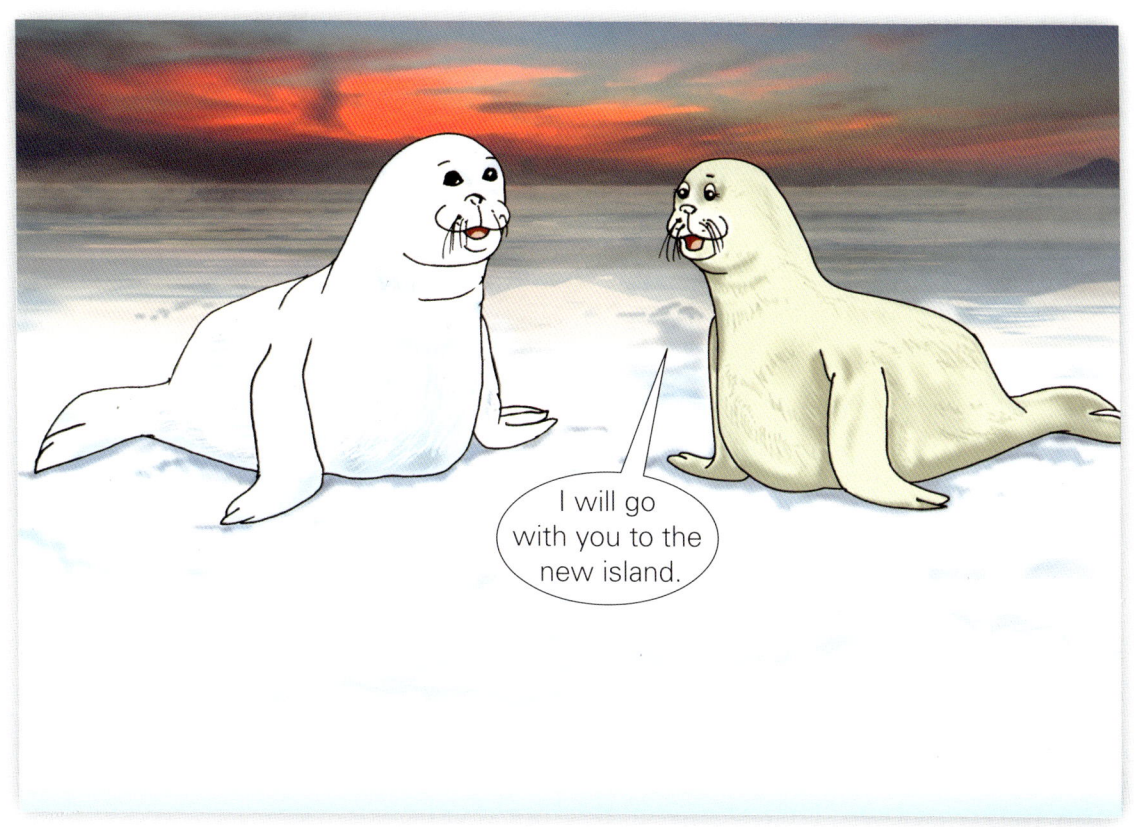

Kotick was very angry. He pounced on the young seal and injured him badly. Lary was watching Kotick fight from a distance and was proud of his strength. She said, "Kotick, I believe you. Once we are married, I will accompany you to the new island."

Kotick thanked Lary and said, "I feel much better now. Please join me for dinner."

After dinner, Kotick announced to his family, "Lary and I will live on the new island after we get married. It is disheartening to know that my parents do not believe me. But Lary trusts and supports me. We will have children and make nurseries for them in a safe place. We do not want to see cruel men kill our babies."

Sea Catch and Matkah realised that Kotick was right. They said, "Well then, we will come with you too."

Sea Catch told his friends that they were going to move to the new island soon. Since most of the seals respected Sea Catch, they decided to follow him to the new island.

The older seals told Kotick, "We are sorry that we did not trust you, Kotick. We have realised our mistake and we want to come too."

Kotick was overjoyed and agreed to take them to the island.

The younger seals decided to follow the older ones for their children's safety.

After several days of swimming, Kotick's family and the other seals came to the new island.

They were delighted to see the new place. They thanked Kotick for his efforts. They praised the island's beauty and the food it provided. It also appeared to be a safe place.

Matkah and Sea Catch were proud of their son.

The seals chose their homes on the beach and made nurseries without any man disturbing them ever again. They were safe and happy at last.

Rikki-Tikki-Tavi

Long ago, there lived a mongoose in a burrow with his parents. His ears and the tip of his nose were pink. His head looked just like that of a weasel. His fur and tail were similar to that of a cat.

One night, it rained heavily and the whole place was flooded.

The water gushed into the mongoose's burrow while he was sleeping inside. Soon he was carried away by the water currents.

To save himself, the frightened mongoose clung to a piece of wood that floated nearby. Then he fainted. When the mongoose regained consciousness after many hours, he found himself lying in the middle of a garden path.

The mongoose was so tired that he could not move. He thought, "How I wish somebody saves me before I die here!"

Just then, a boy named Teddy entered the garden with his mother.

Teddy saw the mongoose and exclaimed, "Mother, look! The poor animal must be dead."

Teddy's mother looked closely at the mongoose and said, "No son! He is alive. We will take him home and nurse him back to health." Teddy was happy. He picked up the mongoose gently and went home. He showed the mongoose to his father. "He is ill. We will take good care of him," said his father, examining the mongoose.

Teddy's father wrapped up the mongoose in cotton wool and took him near the fire to keep him warm. Teddy watched with great interest.

After some time, the mongoose opened his eyes and sneezed. Teddy's mother gave him a piece of raw meat. The hungry animal gobbled it up instantly.

The mongoose felt much better and began jumping across everyone's lap. Then the mongoose sat on Teddy's shoulder.

"He could be a great pet for you," said his father. Teddy liked the idea a lot.

The mongoose went around exploring the house. He liked the place, as he found many things he had never seen before.

The mongoose thought, "I love this place. The peoplc are so nice. I can stay here with them."

That night, the mongoose followed Teddy to the bathroom when he went to brush his teeth. He accidentally fell into the bathtub. But he swam from one end to the other happily.

Teddy felt sorry for the mongoose and took him out and dried him.

Every night, Teddy's parents came to Teddy's room before they went to bed. That night, Teddy's mother was surprised to see the mongoose sitting near her son's pillow. She was very worried.

She said to Teddy's father, "I will send the mongoose away tomorrow morning, as I am scared that he may bite our son."

Teddy's father reassured her, "Don't worry! Teddy will be as safe with the mongoose as he would have been with a pet dog."

Teddy's mother was relieved. She trusted her husband's decision.

The mongoose did not stay for long in Teddy's room. He followed Teddy's father to his study and sniffed the inkpot on the table. His pink nose immediately became blue with ink.

Teddy's father laughed and took him on his lap. He said, "If you are not careful, you will end up hurting yourself."

Then Teddy's father lit a cigar and began to read a book. The restless mongoose could not sit still. He forgot the warning and tried to jump on Teddy's father lap. His nose accidentally touched the cigar and was burnt. He cried out loud in pain, "Rikk-tikk-tikki-tikki-tchk!" Within minutes, Teddy and his mother came to the study room.

Teddy's father said, "This animal has to learn to live in a house."

Teddy said, "I guess he will learn slowly. Why don't we name him Rikki-tikki-tavi because that is how he cries?"

Everyone agreed. Thus, Rikki-tikki-tavi became a member of Teddy's family.

Rikki-Tikki Kills the Snakes

Rikki-tikki-tavi, the mongoose, was Teddy's favourite pet.

One morning, Rikki-tikki met Darzee, the tailorbird, and his wife in the garden. They warned Rikki-tikki to be careful of the cobra, Nag, and his wife, Nagina, who were out of their hole.

"Yesterday, Nag ate one of our babies when he fell down from the nest. Now, they are looking for some other animal to feast on," said Darzee.

Rikki-tikki thanked the birds and said, "My friends, I am not scared of snakes."

Suddenly, he heard a hiss and turned around. He saw Nag sitting before him.

Nag hissed, "I am King Cobra. How dare you come into my territory?"

Rikki-tikki said, "I will stop you from troubling innocent animals!"

Then he leaped forward and attacked Nagina who was sitting next to Nag. Nagina was enraged and wanted to kill Rikki-tikki.

But she was so hurt that she went back into her hole with Nag following her. The tailorbirds were overjoyed and praised Rikki-tikki for punishing Nag and Nagina.

At night, Rikki-tikki caught a rat in the house with his paws. When the rat pleaded for his life, Rikki-tikki took pity on him and let him go.

Please let me go! I have something important to tell you.

The rat said, "I will share an important information with you since you spared my life. Nag and Nagina were at the bathroom drain some time ago."

Rikki-tikki rushed to the bathroom immediately and waited for the snakes. Suddenly, he heard Nag and Nagina hissing inside the drain.

Nagina said, "The mongoose will leave this house once we kill all the people who live here."

Agreeing with her, Nag said, "Nagina, you go back and take care of our eggs while I wait here for the man to come to the bathroom. I will kill him first."

Nag slowly came out of the drain.

Rikki-tikki decided to kill the cobra family as Nag and Nagina wanted to harm Teddy and his parents. Seeing Nag, Rikki-tikki attacked him immediately. They fought with each other for a long time. Finally, Rikki-tikki overpowered Nag and killed him.

Hearing the noise, Teddy's father came to the bathroom with his gun.

He was startled to see Rikki-tikki and the dead snake. Soon Teddy and his mother came to the bathroom as well. Teddy's father said to them, "Rikki-tikki has saved our lives or else the snake would have killed us all."

Teddy and his parents thanked Rikki-tikki for his help.

The next morning, Teddy's father picked up Nag's dead body with a stick and threw it on a pile of garbage. All the animals in the garden thanked Rikki-tikki for killing the cruel cobra.

Rikki-tikki thought, "I must look for Nagina before she comes to take revenge for her husband's death. I must break all her eggs."

The mongoose went looking for Darzee before breakfast. He asked the bird, "Did you see Nagina this morning?" Darzee said, "She is sitting next to her husband's body, mourning his death."

Rikki-tikki asked, "Where has she hidden her eggs?" Darzee was scared, but he pointed towards the melon bed.

Rikki-tikki rushed to the melon bed and broke all the eggs one by one. When he had just one egg left to break, he heard Darzee scream, "Rikki-tikki, I saw Nagina go towards the veranda!"

Carrying the last egg in his mouth, Rikki-tikki reached the veranda. When he saw Nagina, he challenged her.

"I have broken all your eggs in the melon bed. If you want to save this one, fight with me!" cried Rikki-tikki.

Though Nagina was grieving, she fought to save her last egg. But soon she was killed.

All the birds and animals praised Rikki-tikki when he broke the last egg. Teddy and his parents were very proud of him.

Meanings of Difficult Words

The Elephant Dance

employed : hired to work for wages or a salary

yearn : long for something strongly

dishearten : make one lose confidence and hope; discourage

disappointed : sad or displeased

amazing : wonderful

merrily : happily

trample : crush something (or someone) by stepping on it

devastation : great destruction and damage

Sea Catch's Family

sleek : smooth and shiny

speechless	:	unable to speak temporarily, as a result of a shock
experience	:	knowledge and skill gained over a period of time
shallow	:	of little depth
instructions	:	directions; orders

Special Kotick

migrate	:	move from one region or habitat to another, according to the seasons
shearing	:	the process of cutting wool from sheep (or other animals)
retaliate	:	hit back
welfare	:	well-being, health, happiness and good fortune
companions	:	friends
prevent	:	stop something from happening

The Seals Move to Safety

organise : arrange an activity or event

announce : make a formal public statement about a plan or a decision

prowling : moving about restlessly and stealthily

retorted : replied angrily

injured : hurt in an accident or attack

Rikki-Tikki-Tavi

weasel : a small, thin animal with brown fur, short legs and a long tail

consciousness : the state of being awake and aware of one's surroundings

wrap : cover

gobble : eat something quickly and often noisily

trust	:	believe that someone is good and honest
restless	:	unable to rest or relax as a result of anxiety or boredom

Rikki-Tikki Kills the Snakes

territory	:	an area of land or region under a state or ruler
leap	:	jump
enraged	:	very angry; furious
overpower	:	defeat someone with great strength or power
mourning	:	grieving over a big loss
veranda	:	porch or area outside the house, usually partly enclosed
grieving	:	feeling extremely sad